TERMINUS STATION

TERMINUS STATION

JEFF LYONS

Storygeeks
Press

Terminus Station

ISBN: 978-0-578-62975-9 (pbk)

Cover art by Tracy Lyn: www.virtuallypossibledesigns.com

Interior design by Jeff Lyons

Web: www.storygeeks.com

First Edition

Printed in the U.S.A

DEDICATION

This is for loyal readers past, present, and future.
Because without you, what's the point?

ACKNOWLEDGMENTS

The author would like to thank the following individuals for their support, help, encouragement, patience, infinite patience, faith, trust, belief, handouts, generosity, and small petty crimes undertaken to promote the success of this book.

- *Kimberley Heart, David Allan, Linda English, Allison Smith, Josh Melville, Evelyn Pentikis, Rebecca Ingle, Malcom Wong, Jacob Marquez, Caroline Leavitt, and Dorothy Turnbull* —thank you for being trusted beta readers, editors, and telling me the truth.
- *Tracy Lyn*—thank you again, as always, for the great artwork.

Narrative Engine for Any Story

#6: Seven Steps to Busting Writer's Block Forever

CONTENTS

BEST LAID PLANS

To Be or not to be, that is the question—what a cliché, he thought. Random bits like that came to him when he was sleepy. Like tonight, standing on the train platform waiting for the number fifty, he leaned against a support girder near the edge of the platform and danced his usual late-night dance: nodding, starting, nodding again, almost falling, catching himself, wide awake, only to fall back into a hypnogogic haze. That's when the bits came: *Better to have loved and lost, than never to have loved at all —stupid shit*, he thought. *Where's the fucking train, it's midnight?*

Ira seemed always in a rush after leaving work, but when he stopped to think about it, the same truth always hit him: there was nothing to rush home to. He wasn't married, didn't have a girlfriend, no dog or cat or pet of any kind. Nothing living waited for him in his apartment, unless you counted mold on the broccoli in the fridge. He wondered for a moment whether mold was technically living. Anyway, there was no imperative, no pressure, no urgency that stopped him from taking his time and waiting for the next train or from walking upstairs to the street and getting the number eighteen bus. The bus would mean a slow ride home, with stops every other block for the next seven miles. He took it once and decided never again. Too many weirdos late at night. And the buses seemed to have more smells and stains and the suggestive remains of other people's lives left behind in flimsy plastic bags. At least the transit authority kept the trains cleaner and clear of human flotsam. Rush or no rush, he just wanted to get home, to implement his plan.

All this thinking kept him wide awake, as he stood at the edge of the platform at the corner of Humboldt and Mercer streets. He looked down the track for an oncoming light, but there was nothing. So he stepped back behind the yellow zone, with its worn black lettering warning of injury should it be crossed in the presence of a moving train. *Like they really give a shit about me, it's just to cover their asses legally.*

His mind wandered as it wanted to, unfettered by a will or desire or need. Even the plan could not focus his meandering thoughts. But that was probably more out of avoidance than true inability to focus. Even so, Ira's mind was well-trained for meandering. Standing in this very spot, or in a spot near it, day in and day out, every week, every month, every year, had been his custom for the past fifteen years. His whole being was conditioned for this nightly ritual.

Ira worked as an assistant manager at the local Chik-a-Bun Family Restaurant on Seventh and High streets. He had worked his way up the ladder from cleaning crew, to host, to cashier, to waiter, to cook, and then to assistant manager. His climb was not what one might call meteoric, but it was "upward," and "steady," and it followed accepted company promotion guidelines.

Each night he would help the cashier balance out the register, do the same for the bartender, then check the waitresses' and waiters' side work (especially making sure that the contents of any half-empty ketchup and mustard bottles were consolidated into full bottles), walked the cooks' line and make sure that all the grease traps and stovetops were wiped down and the locks secured on all pantry doors, finish totaling up the night's timecards and recorded overtime and fixed missed punches from the time clock, fill out the night's final paperwork and locking all receipts and vendor billings in the safe tucked beneath the cash register, and finally turn on the alarm system and turned off the lights as he left through the backdoor into the parking lot. Every night, Wednesday through Sunday, with Mondays and Tuesdays off. Chik-a-Bun closed at ten, and he was out by eleven-thirty and secure in his spot on the train platform by midnight.

"Routine becomes its own routine, Ira Blechman," his mother, Sophie, had warned many times, not merely to point out the obvious to him but more to bemoan his predictable existence, and express the parental disappointment that must always follow the life of a child devoid of passion or initiative. Ira knew he was a disappointment; no one feels the dull throb of mediocrity like the middling themselves.

The maddening part, though, was that Ira knew what kind of man he was or, more correctly, what kind of man he was not. He had learned to keep ceilings low, horizons close, and any brass rings safely within arm's length. *A man's reach should never exceed his grasp.* That misquoted line from Robert Browning's *Andrea del Sarto* was burned into his soul like a scarring brand, as were the twisted words he learned to use to soothe the wound, *Or what's a hell for?*

Sophie had inflicted that brand many years before, carefully teaching her only son not to run too fast or reach too far. The lessons always entailed a slap, or pinch, or worse. Sophie trained dogs for a living, and the same alpha-dog methods she used on pups, she used on him. Children and dogs have a great deal in common; they both crave love, and their spirits are easily broken. Ira hated dogs.

He had seen his mother that morning because part of his daily routine was stopping at the Rose Kivel Manor Assisted Living facility close to his studio apartment. Sophie had been at the facility for more than a year after having broken her hip by slipping on a banana peel. That's what she liked to tell people when they asked how she came to live there. It always got a laugh, and then the questions stopped. But Ira knew the truth of it. She had broken her hip taking a swing at him, trying to slap some sense into his head after he had turned down an arranged blind date with the daughter of one of Sophie's busy-body friends, "You think girls just grow on trees? You think you are getting younger? Beggars can't be choosers, Ira Blechman. She's settling . . . you should too . . . so, snap out of it!"

But it wasn't as though he hadn't tried: failed businesses, after failed jobs, after failed dreams had all led him to Chik-a-Bun and fifteen years of steadfast sameness. Soul-killing, spirit-deadening, dream-ending: all the clichés applied to him and the dead-end life he lived. His training was deep and automatic. Don't run too fast, don't reach too far, dream in black and white, there's a good dog. But all that would end tonight— with the plan. It was well thought out. It was a good plan. Tonight, he would take a stand for the first time in his life and accomplish something.

The previous week he had bought an old straight razor, well balanced, with a genuine ivory handle, carved—ironically—into the raised image of an elephant. The razor was elegant, expensive, but dull, so he had to find a proper knife sharpener to put the edge back on it. The sharpening took only a few minutes and cost more than the razor itself. That was all right, he'd told himself. It was a single-purpose blade anyway, no point fretting about costs and incidentals. The sharpener, an elderly man from the Punjab and a multi-generational craftsman in the maintenance and upkeep of fine blades, told him to be very careful with the first shave. Ira recalled smiling at that remark as the man showed on him the proper angle, pressure, and speed required to avoid a bloody mess. Ira had nodded politely. "This razor is now so sharp, Mr. Blechman, that if you cut yourself, you would not even feel it." Ira tipped him twenty dollars and quickly left the shop.

Ira's bathroom would be the place, and the time would be his favorite time of day, between 3 a.m. and sunrise. Even in the city, the early morning hours felt calm, quiet, and untroubled by the earthly concerns of the coming day. In the hushed silence of the predawn, he would lie in his bathtub, half-filled with warm water, then use the razor to open his ulnar arteries on both arms, quickly followed by two deep cuts on each of his inner thighs to slice both femoral arteries. He would take care when angling the blade. Arterial tissue was elastic and acted very much like sphincter muscle when injured, pinching itself off to restrict blood loss and potentially dragging out the process well into the morning hours. A thirty-degree cut would be best, making it less likely that the arterial walls would squeeze the cut closed. Simple lidocaine injections delivered at strategic spots on his arms and inner thighs would numb his skin and deep muscles to make the cuts pain-less enough.

One large sheet of black utility plastic, the kind used to line large containers, would be spread around the tub's interior, hanging down around the side of the tub so that the excess could be folded over the plastic used as a makeshift body bag so that he could be moved out of the tub and onto the floor or gurney (assuming paramedics would attend the scene). A small hole would be made in the plastic just above the drain so that the bloodied water might drain before he was lifted out of the tub but not so big a hole that it might make a mess of the whole act. Whoever found him would also find a nicely typed note. Not some maudlin, weepy suicide note quoting metaphysical poetry, or giving soapy good-byes to friends and family, or bidding farewell to the cruel world. There was no one to say goodbye to, least of all his mother, who was only a constant reminder to him that his existence on planet Earth was nothing more than that of a placeholder. She would miss him for a short time because she would lose a familiar point of focus for her vitriol and nastiness. She would find another. Just as when she put down one of her dogs, she would move on to the next pup.

No, the note would be a simple set of instructions, taped to the bathroom mirror, explaining how to fold the plastic properly, how to drain the water, how to rematch the hole, and what phone numbers to call for the city to come and dispose of his remains.

Ira had thought about hanging himself but decided that would be too messy and painful, and the idea of pissing and shitting himself after his bladder and anal sphincter ultimately relaxed left him with a final image of his ending that was neither pitiable, nor dignified. *Am I looking for pity?*—the thought flashed. Not to mention that there was always a chance he might do it all wrong and end up hanging there for a long time slowly asphyxiating, and maybe not even dying, instead becoming a drooling husk in a wheelchair in the room next to his mother's at the Rose Kivel Manor Assisted Living Facility.

He also thought about shooting himself, but there were disturbing statistics about the number of self-inflicted gunshots that missed their marks and only maimed and disfigured their victims. Once again, the odds of the nursing home scenario loomed too heavily against him. And then there was the carbon-monoxide method, a favorite of many. But for that you needed a car, and a garage, and a place to do it that wouldn't attract attention. Ira had no car, or garage, and he lived in a place where such arrangements would be difficult and unpredictable.

No, the razor was the most elegant, noiseless, and painless method. It was a good plan.

THE WOMAN AND THE TRAIN

At that moment Ira sensed a change in the air inside the station and felt the low vibration of the platform signaling an oncoming train. He turned his head slightly toward the uptown tunnel and saw a bright speck of light wobbling and jiggling, hanging in midair as it shone through the dingy, underground darkness. The rumble of the train itself was still barely audible, but the speck caught his eye and grew in intensity. Rather than the usual flickering dull yellow, this light was brilliantly white and strong, like a tiny sun blazing in a starless night. And the thunderous, mechanical racket that always announced a train's arrival into the station was replaced by a hush and whisper of air so gentle that it brushed past his face like the wings of a butterfly, followed by a quiet mechanical hum as the train glided up to the platform to an almost silent stop.

Ira stepped back from the yellow safety zone as he looked at the train. Instead of the expected square-shaped, red- and black-painted cars with dirty windows and covered with graffiti, this train was like something out of a 1920s art deco movie poster. Each of its seven cars had a rounded, aerodynamic shape, with no square edges or angular surfaces. Their bright, unpainted, silver metal skins appeared as clean and fresh looking as any train newly off the assembly line. The cars were like seven huge silver bullets on wheels. Ample windows lined each car, which was warmly lit inside with a cozy yellow light, and each car's interior was free of advertising, public notices, or any of the usual signage common to public transportation. It was then that Ira noticed the strange absence of people on the platform and inside the train. By this time, so close to midnight, a small late-night crowd had always formed to board the last train. But not tonight. Not for this train.

Ira had heard that from time to time, when trains broke down or when maintenance was scheduled, the city sometimes used temporary replacements for cars put out-of-service. But he'd never heard of entire trains being pulled off the line and replaced. He shrugged and figured that there was a first time for everything. He grinned to himself, thinking, *and a last time*.

Ira had to admit there was something eerie about being the only person on the platform about to enter an empty train. But he also experienced an exhilarating feeling of excitement that he could not explain. The look of the thing was so out of the ordinary, so unexpected, that he felt impatient to board the train and get going. *What would come next? How would it feel when it was moving?* Why did he even care about any of this? But none of his musings would mean anything unless one car opened its doors to let him onboard. The train just sat there at the platform humming, still, and shining like a metal jewel.

As if on cue with the completion of his thoughts, one of the car doors slid open, two cars down from where he was standing. No doors opened on any of the other cars, just that one. Ira took a breath and looked up and down the platform again, hoping that another person had shown up to help take the edge off the strangeness of the scene, but he was still alone. He slowly walked down to the open door, checking closely in each car for another living human being—there were none. And then he came to the open car.

He stood in the open doorway and felt suddenly hesitant. His unexplained excitement had changed to caution, perhaps even vigilance. He felt an odd impulse to take care as a primal instinct rose up his spine and spread out across his back like a chilling shroud. *Mind the gap.* He remembered the phrase from years earlier when rode in London's tube system, the warning to step carefully across the space between the platform and the edge of the train's threshold. Ira stared at the gap, confused that his feet were not moving. He couldn't stand there forever. The doors could close at any moment; then he'd have to walk home—all seven miles.

He would have to step inside soon, but something was stopping him; that damned chill. He could almost hear his mother's voice hanging in the stale air of the station, judging him, chiding him, dismissing him for his doubt and hesitancy and indecision. *Get on the damn train, Ira. There's nothing to be afraid of . . . it's just a train . . . you big oaf . . . you loser . . . you hapless cur of son!*

It was then that Ira saw the woman, just out of the corner of his eye, sitting near the end of the car on one of the seats farthest from the door. Her eyes met his, and a big smile spread across her pale white face. She had deep-set, piercing blue eyes and long blond hair that fell loosely around her alabastrine shoulders. As she smiled, fine lines creased at the corners of her mouth and eyes, suggesting she might be close to Ira's age, but there was a youthfulness, an almost a childlike innocence about her demeanor.

Ira never noticed people, not really. How they dressed, how they groomed themselves, how they felt in one's presence. He had no interest. But here he was—noticing. Her clothes looked ordinary enough but struck him as a bit out of date. Ira was no fashionista or clothes horse, so it wasn't his habit to judge such things. But her "look" was curious. She wore a sensible black pencil skirt and white silk top. A simple crew-necked cardigan covered her blouse but was loosely fitting to expose her shoulders, accompanied by a sheer red chiffon scarf and white linen gloves. Lacy-white anklet socks and a pair of simple black flats completed the outfit. And then there was the bra. They were called bullet bras in the 1950s and 60s. Ira remembered lusting over an old studio still of Jayne Mansfield wearing little more than a bullet bra and pair of panties, remarking, "You could put an eye out with those things." This woman was not so crass in her presentation, but the effect was still eye-opening.

Ira became painfully aware that he was staring at the woman, so he broke his gaze and fixed it instead on the seat immediately opposite the train's door. His feet moved across the gap and into the car, and before he knew it he was sitting down. Avoiding eye contact, he looked straight ahead through the open doorway towards the empty platform. But, no sooner had he taken a seat than the woman moved to a seat next to the door on the opposite side of the car, directly in his line of sight. She was still smiling and looking at him with such intensity that he felt no part of him was unseen. Ira had never felt so vulnerable, so obvious.

They sat there, Ira fixated on the newspaper dispenser on the opposite side of the train platform, and she fixated on him, her burning blue-eyed gaze boring through his soul. *Why won't the damn doors close?* Ira thought, and then shouted in his head, *Get me the fuck out of here.*

"The train won't leave quite yet. We'll be awhile, I

think," she said, the smile on her face melting into an easy grin. Her eyes were no longer dissecting him; she just gazed at him the way anyone might. Her comment gave Ira pause; had he mumbled his thoughts under his breath? *How did she know——?*

"It's considered rude to stare at strangers," he scolded her.

She got up and sat next to him on the long seat; it was not the response Ira had expected. He scooted to the side a bit to open some distance between them, but the arm rail stopped him. He thought about getting up and moving, but—he didn't.

"What's the train waiting for?" he said. "We should be on our way by now."

"It's waiting for you," she replied. "But these things can't be rushed." Finally she looked away from him and down into her lap.

"For me?" Ira asked. "But I'm sitting right here."

"Waiting for you to . . . promise to come back."

"I'm here every night," he scoffed. "Kind of silly to make promises."

"A promise is sacred. A promise holds consequences. A promise is a bond." Her tone was firm, but patient, as if she was explaining something to a five-year-old. Ira resisted the knee-jerk reaction to get snippy and condescending.

Before he could make some awkward comeback, she asked, "Are you in a hurry to get home?"

"As a matter of fact, yes."

"Really?"

What a strange thing for her to ask. Had she detected traces of his motive, his plan? But it was her tone, more so than words, that made Ira feel unmasked. "What? Why did you say that?" He spoke defensively. What was it about this woman that made him feel so outside himself?

Ignoring his question completely, she lifted a limp, white-gloved hand for a shake. "I'm Lily."

Ira gathered several of her fingertips into a bunch and shook them loosely. The linen of her gloves felt over-starched and stiff. "Ira." He knew his handshake was the kind other men belittled. Well, everyone really.

When Ira spoke his name, Lily's eyes lit up, and her big, broad smile rose again like a sun breaking a night's dark horizon. No one had ever smiled at him like that. Ira half expected her to break into tears of sheer joy at the sound of his name. "Ira…"

"Yes," he said weakly.

"You can let go of my fingers now." She giggled.

He hadn't realized he was still shaking her hand. "Oh, yeah . . . stupid me…"

"No, not stupid," she said pointedly. "Never stupid. You just need sleep. This can be draining."

"What can be draining?" he asked, his confusion growing.

"The train has decided to leave now. You should go home." Lily pulled away a bit to make to make room for Ira to leave.

"But I haven't promised," Ira retorted. "What about that?" Now he was getting snippy.

Lily did not react or become defensive; she merely smiled. "This is so. Would you like to come back? Would you like to talk again?"

"Yes." The word escaped his mouth before he even knew it. *What the hell*, he thought.

"Come back tomorrow night, same time. Don't be late. I'll be waiting." Lily's voice was reassuring and solid.

"You're telling me to get off the train?" Ira was incredulous.

She nodded. "You have a long walk, right?"

"What if I don't? What if I just sit here?" He was being argumentative and petulant, and it took him a moment for him to realize he was a reacting to fear. He was afraid to leave the train. He was afraid to go home. Earlier, that was all he could think about, but now—

"Tomorrow night. Same time. Don't be late . . . Ira dear." Lily whispered the word "dear" the way a mother would to her child. It was more than unexpected; it took the air out of him like a deep squeeze from a too-strong hug. With a single word he was disarmed and undone. The closeness, intimacy, caring, and sense of being known that flowed out of her simple words made him weak in the knees. *Who is this?*

He found himself on his feet and shuffling weakly to the open car door. He didn't remember getting up.

Just before he exited the car, Lily called out to him. "Promise?"

"Yes," he replied.

She beamed, then removed one of her lacy gloves and threw it to him in the doorway. "We're so happy. Take this, you'll need it. Bring it back with you. Now go." Her voice was urgent for the first time.

From the moment he stepped onto the train, it was Ira, not Lily, who had been off-balance. But now, in Lily, he detected a note of vulnerability to match his own. Sensing she needed something from him gave him strength. He stood up taller. "Lily, I will."

Ira, never taking his eyes off her, backed off the car and onto the platform. No sooner had his body passed through the open doorway than Lily gave a wry smile and said, "It's not a good plan, Ira. It's a terrible plan. And remember, this is how it is; how it has always been. How it will always be."

Then the doors closed in a whisper in front of him. The train pulled forward and disappeared, too quickly, into the black hole of night.

THE COLD LIGHT OF DAWN

The girl with the blue eyes knew about the plan. *But how?* Ira wondered. She told him the plan was bad. Not just bad—terrible. Had he mentioned the razor, the plastic, the note? Did he speak of the razor and the plastic? In his befuddled and clumsy moments with Lily, had he unconsciously revealed his hand, like a pathetic amateur gambler unable to muster a basic poker face? He was sure he had not, and yet . . . and yet her last words. *This is how it is; how it has always been. How it will always be.* What kind of nonsense was that?

She seemed even to know the train's intentions, as if some drama of her own was unfolding, with him an unwitting bit player. But how? As if trains could want something. All of this could not have been random chance or coincidence. It was too specific, too personal. Too targeted at him. *Why ask why, Ira Blechman,* he heard his mother chiding him in the back of his mind. *Shit happens, and that's all that ever happens to us Blechmans.*

"Shut up, Mother!" Ira burst out. A wave of embarrassment and shame rolled through him, and he half-expected a solid, full-handed slap to knock him backward in penalty for his endless questioning. But there was no one to hear, no punishment coming. The night-streets were deserted.

Ira thought about calling a cab or texting a rideshare, but he walked—all seven miles. He wanted time to think. There were dots to connect, mysteries to solve, questions to plan for the next encounter. And there would be a next time. Lily had made that clear. Who was this woman? How did she know him?—and know him she did, he felt it in his bones. What was her connection to that strange and beautiful train? And why him?

That last question surprised Ira more than any other. He had the feeling they had chosen him. *That's ridiculous*, he knew, and yet the entire time he'd been on the train, he felt like the guest of honor at some weird party.

Ira had been too unnerved by Lily's attentions and her beguiling eyes to realize the truth. But now, slogging through pitch-black streets and bad neighborhoods, he gleaned it—he was meant to find that train, he was meant to meet Lily, and he was expected to return to both. *Expected by whom, by what?* There was no answer to that question, nor to the dozens of other questions swirling through his mind. Ira was a leaf on some strange aetheric wind blowing him toward some end, the nature of which he did not understand.

He arrived home in the predawn morning, a time when even a busy city was still subdued by stillness and quiet and the dark blanket of night. He made his way up to his apartment, careful not to disturb the hushed, dead air that filled his building's hallways and that followed him into his room.

As he prepared for bed, Ira realized that he was wide awake and nowhere near sleep. The long walk, rather than exhausting him, had filled him with a buzzing from his head to his toes. It wasn't until this moment, sitting on his bed, barefoot and energized, that he realized he had not once thought about the plan. The thing that had only hours earlier had consumed him and his consciousness was now like a distant, fading image. He remembered the razor, the plastic, the detailed instructions taped to the bathroom mirror describing how to wrap, contain, and dispose of his remains with the least exertion possible. *ALIVE*. The word rang in his head, and then even louder, like the bells of a cathedral announcing the splitting open of Heaven and the descent of the angles, its second syllable: *LIVE*.

Ira pulled down the note from the bathroom mirror, crumpled it up into a tight ball, and threw it into the wastebasket. He then took the roll of plastic sheeting from behind the door and tucked it away in the utility closet next to the bathroom. Finally, he removed the pristine and glistening razor blade from its protective cover and watched the light from the bathroom ceiling bouncing off it in flashes and bursts of reflected light. The blade found its way back into its holster and then into a small drawer under the sink: at the back of the drawer where things could be forgotten.

Later, lying in bed, Ira stared at the ceiling, unable to sleep. He thought about taking a sleeping pill, a strong prescription his mother had arranged for him from one of her many doctors, but sleep was not what he wanted. What he wanted was to understand what had happened. All he could think of was the strange, beautiful woman with the intense blue eyes that looked right through him and the silver train with no passengers save her. And—if he returned the following night, he could see her again. No, there was no "could," there was only the certainty that he would. She had said so, she foresaw it! As silly as it seemed, the feeling that his future had been cast was unmistakable. He would see the woman on the train again, and there was nothing on this Earth that would change that fact. Ira had never been as clear about the outcome of anything as he was about this, and he had to admit that there was a sweet vulnerability in knowing that he had no choice but to comply. Lying there staring up into a shapeless void, his eyes followed the faint and shadowy impression of a small ceiling fan as it turned above him. As he slipped away, at last, into a black, dreamless sleep, he smiled and realized, *the plan had changed.*

Ira woke to a distant sound—a beeping noise. It took a moment or two for him to orient and return from wherever his consciousness had fled the night before, to make sense of all that had happened: the woman, the train, the weirdness. Had any of it really happened? Ira was frankly unsure. He didn't dream, he never dreamed, but he remembered what had happened. Maybe this was his first dream? But how could he know the difference between a memory and a dream if he'd never had a dream before? Then he remembered: *the glove.* Lily had given him one of her gloves, "You'll need it," she had told him. "Bring it back with you." She knew he'd question himself, doubt his own mind. Lily gave him proof that it had happened. That he wasn't dreaming.

Ira grew irritated by the low beeping sound in the background, but he had a bigger priority: the glove. Where had he put it? He shuffled out of bed and retraced his movements since his long walk home. Nothing in the foyer, or on the kitchen table, or in the bathroom. He searched the floors in each section of his studio to see if he had dropped it: nothing. Despondent, he looked back into his bedroom. *Is it possible?* Ira threw back the covers, then the sheets: nothing. With tentative fingers he pulled on the corner of one of his pillows and flipped it over to reveal the sheet beneath. A single, white linen glove lay crumpled there, just where he had put it before vanishing into sleep. Lily's glove had lain beneath his head throughout his slumber. Ira had never slept with anyone, but he wondered if what he was feeling in that moment was what a man feels when he sleeps with a woman. The idea sent a reflexive flinch through him and he winced and glanced over one of his shoulders, half expecting—.

It was then he realized that the beeping noise had stopped, that it was his answering machine announcing that he messages, lots of messages. *Odd*, he thought. *No one ever called—except.* Seventeen messages played back, all time-stamped for that morning, during the hours he had slept. Not from his mother, but from her doctor. "Ira, you need to get over to Saint Bartholomew's right away. I don't know how much longer she has."

THE LADY SAID DON'T BE LATE

Saint Bartholomew's Hospital was one of those institutions that looked more like a fortress than a place of healing. Built in an age when concrete and solidity were considered more attractive than glass and transparency, Bartholomew's was a big-city trauma center, a place where people went to die from gunshots, knife wounds, and overdoses. If the dead walked the Earth, the hallways of this place would be teeming with them.

Ira entered the cavernous main lobby, wading through a sea of indigent and wasted humanity. Fading murals, painted in the 1930s during the Roosevelt administration, lined the walls, depicting powerful doctors and nurses wielding stethoscopes, scalpels, and tongue depressors like weapons to vanquish sickness and decrepitude. This was a war lost long ago. Around him, in hushed and desperate tones, several languages were being spoken, none of them English. Amid anonymous whimpers, groans, and coughs, Ira approached the main desk and the grim, thickly armored police officer who was screening visitors.

"I'm here to see a patient," Ira said.

"Room number?" asked the officer without looking up.

"Um . . ." His mother's doctor hadn't told him the room number.

The officer looked up, annoyed. "Patient name?"

"Blechman, Sophie."

The man turned to a computer monitor that cast a pale, deadening light across his face, washing out any color or human warmth. His pudgy fingers hunted and pecked on the keyboard for a long while. "1002, tenth floor, elevators are to the right. Take off your shoes."

"What?" Ira was mystified, but he started to take off his shoes as ordered.

The officer yelled, "Not here, you idiot." He pointed to a long queue for the elevators where a line of shoeless visitors waited their turns at an airport-like security area complete with metal detectors and screeners. Ira, a shoe in each hand, shuffled over to the line and waited.

❧

Twenty minutes later he was on the tenth floor, hunting for room 1002. The hustle and bustle of nurses, doctors, and orderlies mirrored the chaos far below in the lobby. The din of beeping machines, loudspeaker announcements, and hushed hallway conversations betrayed any hope of a restful recuperation, let alone a quiet bedside chat between a patient and loved one.

And then Ira saw it: "1002" in thick black lettering above an open door. A sickly, green-yellow glow of bad florescence seeped from the room like pus from an open sore. Ira stepped forward and then stopped. What if he didn't go into the room? What if he just turned and left? After all, he had promised Lily he would meet her that night, and she'd been clear: don't be late. Did he really want to risk that? How bad a son would it make him to turn tail and never come back? He knew the answer.

His mother might not even be conscious. And if she were, did he really want to listen to her insults and harangues about his being late, being irresponsible—being him? *Now, is my chance*, he thought. But he hesitated, just for a moment, to let the guilt pass. *He who hesitates is lost.* As the words flashed through his mind, a steady, firm hand grasped his shoulder from behind and held him in place. His mother's doctor faced him, "Good, you're finally here. She's been asking for you."

Room 1002 had three beds but only one patient. His mother was in the farthest bed from the doorway. The lights were dimmed, and the curtains were drawn to seal out any fresh air, light, or prying eyes. The doctor briefed Ira on his mother's condition. "She had a series of mini-strokes throughout last night. She's blind in her left eye. Her left side is paralyzed, and she can't walk. There may be some bleeding in the brain, but we're doing more tests to see exactly where and to what degree. Your mother's in a serious condition. You should be prepared for the worst."

Ira stiffened. "You said she'd been asking for me, so . . ."

The doctor looked at him, perfectly understanding the real question he was asking. "Yes. She can speak, but barely." He turned on his heel and left the room without another word, leaving Ira alone with the machines, IVs, and bad lighting.

Ira stepped slowly toward the farthest bed, hoping against hope that his mother was unconscious. She wasn't. Her watery, bloodshot eyes gazed up at the ceiling in a blank stare through half-open lids. Her lips trembled, as did her hands. A catheter with bag hung from the side of the bed, half filled with golden liquid tinged with blood. The pungent smell of bodily fluids mixed with medicines and medicinal salves assaulted his sense of smell. He covered his nose and mouth with his hand.

He stood by her bed, not saying a word. He waited for her eyes to find him, which they did. She locked her gaze on his and her focus and intensity sent a searing shock of humiliation through him. This was her look, her gaze, the one he had grown up with, the one that haunted him still. It was the gaze of a mother for whom giving birth was merely a biological act. Like a small mammal caught in the vice-grip of an anaconda, Ira waited for the black maw of her being to consume him. But the grip he felt was not her soul crushing his, but her hand, which had somehow found his, her icy fingers had closed around his like a trap. Ira could have pulled away, but what kind of son would do that to his dying mother, in a hospital? She had him. Her eyes closed, Ira watched as a satisfied smile crept up the still-supple side of her half-frozen face. He wanted to scream, he wanted to run, but neither was an option given his circumstances. He knew he had to just tough it out and wait for her to fall sleep or—.

As Ira sat dutifully by his mother's side, the long shadows of a setting sun gave way to a starless night devoid of warmth, or magic, or the mystery that night was supposed to promise. His fingers had gone white from her icy grip. His joints ached, and his back needed a long stretch of relief. He must have dozed off asleep in his chair because he suddenly became aware that the doctor stood opposite him, filling out a form. Ira looked at his mother's face. It was pale, bloodless, and dead. Yet, that grip.

"Oh, that," chuckled the doctor. "Muscle spasm turned to rigor mortis. I might need to break her fingers to get you out . . . sorry for your loss, kid."

Ira made his way out of the hospital the same way he had come in, through the crushing horde of humanity in the lobby. He tried to feel something but felt only a fog of emotion. In the cab ride home, he tried to quiet his nerves and to let come whatever feelings or thoughts or ideas might be hidden in the fog. Mother was dead. He was free. What did that mean? Then came a sliver of fear. No, not fear. Dread. *Of what?* he wondered? *Being alone* came the reply. Every slave has his master. But not now, not Ira. He was alone, wholly, unquestionably alone. Then something else emerged from the fog. Slowly a shape, then a face, and then eyes, piercing blue. "Lily," he shouted out loud. The cabby jumped at the noise.

"Are you all right, sir?"

"What time is it?" Ira asked desperately.

"Nearly midnight, sir."

Don't be late, was her warning. "Humboldt and Mercer . . . as fast as you can. I'll pay extra! GO!"

The cabby hit the gas and Ira flew to Lily. He was not alone, not tonight. Not if he could outrun time itself.

At exactly one minute before midnight, the cab arrived. Ira threw a pocket full of bills at the cabby and ran up the stairs to the train platform. He heard the wind moving from the train's movement, heard the hushed whisper of its sparking wheels over the polished rails. He was on time. It was just arriving. He would tell Lily everything. His fog would lift, and she would hear him, all of him. There was no reason for him to believe this would all come to pass, but somehow he knew it would. All he needed was to get on the train.

When he reached the platform panting, gasping for air, it was empty. He was late, just a few seconds too late. The train was leaving the station. Ira ran to the edge of the platform and looked down the tracks to the last car. Standing in the window of the car's vestibule door was a lone figure, two hands reaching up, fingers spread wide on the glass, and a pair of intense blue eyes watching him as the train disappeared into the blackness.

THE MAN AND THE TRAIN

The following days were a blur. Ira stumbled through his life avoiding work, dodging calls from the hospital and funeral home, barely eating or sleeping. Sophie Blechman, the one anchor of his life that had grounded him in something of this Earth, was gone. He should have been making funeral arrangements, organizing a wake, and looking into estate documents. Sophie's friends surely they would want to reach out, to give and seek solace and support. Ira should be on the phone, politely telling them that she was in a better place, listening to their thoughts and prayers, hearing how sorry they were for his loss. He should be thinking of his mother and their life together, reminiscing, remembering the past with all its good and bad. Because no one is all good or all bad, because we're all some combination of the two, and because his mother was only human, so there had to be some good inside her, hidden away deep in some crevice or crack of her being. All these things and more he knew he should be doing.

Instead, he was holding a razor blade in his hand and looking at his thin, distorted reflection in its shiny chrome edge. It was the same blade he had secreted away barely days earlier, quietly sliding it into the back of a drawer where forgotten things lay in wait. Some things demand to be remembered. Some things insist on fulfilling their purpose, on realizing their destiny. Ira held his destiny in his fingers, balancing it just so, perfectly weighted, ready to free himself from all the shoulds, musts, and oughts of this life, to sever his final bonds to the past, to the world, to existence itself. This was always the plan, and now things had come full circle.

And then something caught his eye. A flash of pure white, small, out of place in a room of grays and browns and deep shades of military green. *The glove*, Ira remembered. He had left it where he had found it, on his bed, near his pillow, next to where he dreamed. Like some long-lost message in a bottle, Lily had given him this reminder of her realness. The glove was like a magical talisman. Just holding it returned him to that first night on the train, with all its otherworldly eccentricity and surprising intimacy and closeness. Before Lily, those feelings had been so alien to Ira, so long denied him. But he felt them then—though it seemed like a billion years ago. Lily was reminding him, in this moment at the crossroads, once again, that he was human, that he deserved—should not be denied—that which others take for granted: the simple act of human compassion.

Or was he romanticizing, blowing things out of proportion? Wasn't Lily just a strange little woman who gave him her glove for no reason? Wasn't he inflating his own fantasies, what his many therapists called his wish fulfillment, his hopeful projection onto a world devoid of any desire to see him fulfilled in any way? Because, as he well knew, *the universe doesn't give a fuck.*

And yet *this glove.* A part of him was making the solid argument that he should go back to the plan, line the tub with plastic, fill it with warm water, light some scented candles, and slip away. It would be so easy. But another part, the part that had looked into those fierce blue eyes, that had felt exposed and helpless, that had taken the glove and promised to return, was arguing, was pleading, for him not to give in to himself. *Don't be late*, rang in his ears. *Don't be late.*

And then he knew, by granting him with this little piece of cloth, Lily was giving him a second chance. Tonight was the night; tonight at midnight he had one more chance to right his wrongs and fight for his life. All obstacles were gone, all objections silenced, all excuses played out. All he had to do was return the glove.

～

Ira spent the remainder of the day sitting on the train platform at Humboldt and Mercer streets. There was no way he would miss the train tonight. The throngs of commuters came and went, wary security staff eyed him first with suspicion and then, as the hours passed and it became clear that he posed no threat to anyone, with indifference. The long shadows of the afternoon melted into deepening shades of color until night descended and pushed out any hint of natural light. As night settled against the world, the people coming and going grew fewer and fewer, until the platform was empty, just like that first night—and Ira waited, glove in hand.

Alone on the platform, he could not quiet his mind. All the things he wanted to say to Lily, all the apologies, the I'm-sorries and the conversational ice-breakers, the ones he'd learned in the "Customer Service 101" training class at Chik-a-Bun's employee training so many years before, filled his mind like disembodied voices. But Ira knew what he would probably do. When that train door slid open and his eyes met hers, he would just stand there dumbstruck and frozen in fear that Lily would simply snatch away her glove and kick him off her train without so much as a thank-you. He deserved that. He had that coming. He needed to man up, and just take his medicine, just let the chips fall, or utter whatever stupid mea culpa cliché popped into his head at that moment.

As these voices raged, a barely perceptible rush of air wafted across the cold concrete and slowly built into a gentle gust, declaring that it was time. The intense light from the train's lead car at first blinded Ira, then flashed past him as the train silently arrived at the station. Like the first night, all the cars were empty, but well-lit with a warm, inviting light. The sleek, metal exterior gleamed as if it had been newly washed, and it reflected the station's interior like a polished chrome mirror. Ira stood up and tentatively approached the edge of the platform, the same place he had stood that night. And once again as if on cue, the train stopped exactly where it had stopped then, and two cars down from where he was standing, the door opened—Lily's car.

A shard of panic cut through him; he wanted to run. His survival instincts told him there was danger, but that was just the past pushing its way back into the present, Sophie Blechman reaching out from inside whatever refrigerated box she occupied, pointing a bony finger of blame and guilt and judgment. *Not today, Mother.* Ira was not willing to step backwards—ever again. He walked to the open door and stood, glove in hand, and looked in, expecting to see Lily. But she was not there.

The shard cut again: *Did she leave? Did I screw this up again?* His heart sank. He slowly scanned the empty car—nothing, no one. And then in the middle of the car, lying alone under the seats, he saw a shoe, one of Lily's flats, stuffed with a lacy anklet sock. Ira stepped into the car and walked toward the shoe. He reached down and picked it up with shaking hands. Then he saw

Lily's silk white top and that Jayne Mansfield bra, now scuffed and torn, lying nearby.

He looked to the end of the car and saw her crumpled in a bloody heap, open wounds, bruises the size of melons, blood-soaked thighs, fractured bone pushing up through skin. Her face was a pulp of raw tissue and coagulated ichor. He covered the distance between them in an instant and knelt down beside her. He didn't know her; she was a stranger, an unknown and impenetrable being, yet he could not hold back tears. The pain and loss and grief he couldn't feel for his own mother, he felt for this stranger. He cried in the face of such cruelty and death. Who could do such a terrible thing? That night he'd been late, someone else must have taken his place. Another, an interloper, had violated Lily's world and then her. In a life filled with nothing but bad choices and missed opportunities, surely this was the worst. Surely he was the worst?

Just as Ira was about to fling himself into utter despair, he witnessed a miracle. Lily's bruised and battered chest lifted in a weak breath. He instinctively looked to her face, such as it was. A single, swollen, purple lid was cracked open, and the bloodshot eye beneath, with its pure blue iris, looked deeply into him. Lily was alive. Ira gently lifted her into an embrace. She whimpered in pain as he brought her head close to his ear. He did not speak, but she did. "Ira . . ."

"Lily . . .," he answered.

" . . . love me." It was a command.

As she uttered those two words, the car doors closed and the train silently slid from the station as if on a whisper.

～

Time and space are combined into a single dimension in physics, Ira thought. *Now I know why.* Since he had stepped onto the train and found the wreck of Lily lying on the floor, time-space was indeed unified. Ira had no sense of either. Outside the train, the world (if there was a world) blurred and morphed into something that appeared to be moving but not moving. Time must have passed, but Ira had no sense of how quickly or how slowly. All he knew was that he had spent whatever time had passed in a state of physical bliss. He and Lily had spoken no further words. Only their bodies had spoken, through touches and caresses, in pain and pleasure.

Ira had never been with a woman. None had ever invited him to. But when one finally did, he was shocked at how easily it came to him, how familiar, easy, primal, and undeniable. He didn't know how many minutes, or hours, or even days they had spent silently embracing, but after some span of space-time, Ira noticed the changes. The most broken parts of Lily were healing. Fractures, once protruding and bleeding, retracted and set; lacerations deep and oozing sealed; black, blue, and purple contusions lightened into the translucent alabaster of her skin; and those swollen and bloody orbs that had been her eyes became the same intense blue windows into his soul that he had felt on that first night.

It was all impossible. Lily, the train, the healing before his eyes, surely all of it was from some disturbed hallucination. But there he was, in the middle of it, not as observer but as participant. As if he were in some strange lucid dream, knowing that he was dreaming but could choose to wake at will, Ira felt present for the first time in his life, and if this was a waking dream, then he did not want it to end. But something told him that it was a prelude to some crescendo yet to come. He had his part to play, and so did Lily. As they lay woven together on the floor of the car, Ira realized it was time to ask the question.

"Did someone else come, that night, when I didn't? Did they do this to you?" He trembled as he spoke.

She shook her head no, then whispered, "You know who did this."

"How could I know?"

Lily sat up and shivered a bit at the cold that had crept into the car. Ira heard the heaters turn on, as if reacting to her shivering. A warm flow of air pushed away the cold, bringing the car to a comfortable temperature. She reached around in the dim light, searching for her clothes. The lights of the car brightened just enough to reveal where every stitch of clothing lay. As Lily slowly dressed, she said "You know, it took you some time to piece it together. But you have it now."

Once again, she was right. From the moment he had stepped into this impossible place he knew. It wasn't the clear kind of knowing you get from solving a problem or reading a book; it was more like the muddy foreknowledge you feel just before stepping through a darkened doorway, or taking that shortcut through a back alley in the worst part of town. More lies ahead than you might expect, or want, but you go anyway.

Pieces of the dream showed themselves. Every whim, every cue, every expectation, and every anticipation Lily formed, the surroundings dutifully fulfilled. She wanted a door to open; it opened. She wanted the train to leave; it left. She wanted heat; she got heat. The train, like some companion of metal and plastic and glass, heard every request and responded accordingly. But Ira sensed that the train wasn't just doing her bidding—no, it was choosing to do so of its own free will. And if it could choose to make her warm, and comfortable, and safe, it could choose not to not do those things. Ira repeated her words to himself, *You know who did this.*

"Why am I here?" he asked.

"To release me." Her reply was matter-of-fact, an irrefutable truth.

"Why me?" Ira truly did not know.

"Because you were the one who showed up. And

you came back. More than anything, Ira—you came back."

"That's what 'don't be late' was all about." He was seeing. "Making sure I'd come back."

She smiled and kissed his cheek with a gentle brush of her gloved hand. "Don't be silly. You had to want to come back. You have to want to stay." Lily looked deeply into him. "You understand what I am saying, don't you? We can't make you do anything."

We? The woman and the train were connected. How, he did not know. Why was an even more impenetrable question than how. But he understood; soon it would not be the woman and the train, but the man. Soon he would be connected, too.

"Yes." She smiled, "You do understand."

She pulled him close and kissed him. It was like a kiss of wind coming off a verdant field in the height of spring, full of Earth, lush grass, and flowering things. The wind swirled around him, caressing his skin, ruffling his hair, and filling his lungs with a breath that was not his own. Without lifting her kiss, Lily, in a low whisper—or was it even her—spoke to Ira. "You belong to us—"

WHERE MONSTERS COME FROM

In the scary stories Ira read as a boy, the tellers of the tales seldom explained where the monsters came from. The ghosts or beasts or malevolent forces who wrought havoc just emerged from somewhere, unseen yet seen, flitting in and out of peripheral vision, lurking inside the tricks of light and shadow cast by sun and moon, or slinking between reflections from cracked window panes or old corroded mirrors. We needn't know where the monsters come from. We need only know how to overcome them, if they can be overcome. And if they can't, then we must learn not to live in fear—another form of victory, another kind of overcoming, even at the expense of our souls.

Whether the train qualified as a monster, or if Lily was its pawn or puppet master, Ira didn't know. They seemed inseparable, conjoined at levels he could not fathom. He spent a great deal of time, if time was even a measurable thing in this place, thinking about those last minutes, or hours, or whatever interval separated one point of being from the next.

When the doors closed, and the train pulled away, Ira felt the sudden, unsettling presence of another. Many hands held him, not just hers. Cold hands, rough hands, hands with blood on them: her blood. And then, as if all the hands granted some distant permission, Lily released him and backed away. No longer was he embraced, but he was held fast. When panic welled up, seeing Lily's face soothed and calmed him. It was then he knew, that, thanks to him, she was released.

Something that was touching him reached deep inside him flipping switches, adjusting cells, rearranging his biology to better fit into this new world he would inhabit. Ira wondered, as his reinvention proceeded, whether he was now a monster and would, someday, have to explain himself.

It was then that the train slowed. Lights turned up bright, and it stopped at a station Ira had never seen. Lily smiled. "This is Terminus Station. It's time for me to leave, Ira."

"Stay," he begged her.

"No."

Without hesitating, she stepped through the door and onto the platform. Before, she had seemed out of place, as though she had stepped straight from the noirish pages of a second-rate 1940s crime novel. Now, standing on the platform, Lily fitted in perfectly. Wherever this time and place was, it was her place, her time.

Before the door closed, Ira burst out, "I love you."

Lily faced him and smiled. "I know."

"What kind of answer is that?" he shot back, angry and not a little rejected.

"An honest one."

The door closed, and the train slipped away silently. Ira watched the window as Lily walked down the platform to the stairs and then disappeared into the station's depths.

The train made its run, back and forth, back and forth between the yard and nowhere in particular. Never stopping, gliding past station after station. He and the train would often pass Lily's station, her terminus. Ira always looked, always hoping, never spotting her. Inside the train, hours passed. Or years? He never really knew until he looked out the windows. Outside time ran on a different clock. Buildings rose and fell; crowds came and went on the platforms. Hats were in, then out. Hemlines up then down. Even the train platforms morphed and changed. Ordinary billboards gave way to digital holograms. Turnstiles scanned for facial recognition. And yet, in the train, time stood still, or very close to it.

It was during one of the usual runs, while passing

through Lily's station, he glimpsed a woman with white gloves and brilliant blue eyes. Slightly older, clothes a bit more modern, walking with purpose, as if on her way to work or a professional appointment. She did not look up at the passing train. No one did. But Ira knew who it was.

And so he glimpsed her, not every day, or week, or even year, but regularly enough that Ira, from his regular perch on the train, always watched for her. Each time he passed her, she had ever-so-slightly changed, had altered along with her time: now a part of life, no longer separate from it. He lived for these moments, these unpredictable reminders that there was a world outside his world where people were born, went to school, had jobs, went to war, kissed, laughed, and did all the human things people do in time and space and life.

And then an extraordinary event occurred. His train passed through Lily's station. It was late at night, and just a few patrons stood scattered along the platform. And Lily stood in her usual spot, but there was a man with her. He was older, mustached, well dressed. They held hands and talked intimately, as if exchanging secrets. From behind them two children stepped into view, poking each other, ignoring their surroundings, engrossed in tormenting one another the way siblings do.

Time slowed, motion blurred, and for a moment Lily broke away from the man and the children and looked at a passing phantasm no one else could see. Her eyes widened as she tried to glimpse it, glimpse him. Ira ran back through the cars, frantically trying to make eye contact with her before the train passed the platform. And it was there, standing in the last car's vestibule, his hands pressed against the window glass, that her eyes met his in an instant of time that hung heavy and immovable. Her lips moved to form two syllables that anyone watching could easily discern—but no one else saw, only him. *Thank you.*

The train sped past the last inches of the platform and into the night, and then he was gone.

That was so long ago. How long? Ira had stopped counting time. The world outside his world had grown so different that he had lost all interest in its strangeness. It was a city, but not his city. It was a civilization, but no longer his. Somehow, though, even as technology advanced and new replaced old, trains, tracks, and stations remained essential. He and the train carried on down the tracks, passing stations in the night, year after year, decade after decade, time after time. Never again did he see Lily, and never again did he make contact with another human being. It was just he, and the train, cheating time.

And then the train stopped. The shock of this event disoriented him and sent that old, familiar shard of panic through him, the same panic someone had infected so long ago, someone he could now barely remember. He and the train stood still at a platform he didn't recognize, at a time he couldn't discern as present, past, or future.

He turned to the door as it slipped open. The platform was dimly lit. In the background, swallowed up by night, bad lighting flickered. *What is it about train stations and bad lighting?*

As the door stood open, a breath of fresh air entered the car—the first breeze he had felt in untold ages. His lungs filled with fresh air, his hair rustled from the gush of wind, and his skin tingled at the first touch of something that was not the train's metal, glass, and plastic.

Ira's mind stretched back to that night when he had stood on the other side of that same gaping door, sweaty, twitchy, and wanting to step through it but unable to. The sense of being drawn and repelled at the same time had to be the strangest sensation of all. Lily had saved him from "the plan," and he had saved her from the purgatory of this place—now his place. *The circle ends where it begins and begins where it ends. Give to get, get to give.* His mind ran through the clichés. Whatever hapless, loose end of humanity that stepped through the door, Ira knew his circle would be complete. Ira knew that they would step whether they wanted to or not, whether they knew they needed to or not. Just as he had, just as Lily had. From across a dark, distant space Lily's words echoed. *This is how it is; how it has always been. How it will always be.*

A lone, wide-eyed woman stood in the doorway, tenuous, confused, half-in, half-out of time. He looked at her and their eyes met. She smiled, reassured, apparently, to have a friendly face to offset the weirdness she sensed was about to engulf her. Ira smiled back. Not because the woman needed reassurance, or comfort, or protection. No, he smiled back for the same reason Lily had smiled at him on that night so long ago. Because he could hear the scream behind her eyes, and because he felt her loose end and his merge into a perfect circle.

Buy Other Titles Here:

http://www.storygeeks.com

DID YOU LIKE THIS BOOK? THEN, I NEED YOU ...

Without reviews, indie books like this one are almost impossible to market.

If you purchased this book on any of the online book outlets, leaving a review will only take a minute and it will be incredibly helpful to me—and other readers.

The truth is, VERY few readers leave reviews. Please help me by being the exception.

Thank you in advance!

Jeff

W elcome to thirteen minutes of suspense! This excerpt is from my novella *13 Minutes*, a scifi-horror, suspense novella. Enjoy, as you piddle your pants a little in fear.

~

13 MINUTES
a novella by Jeff Lyons

Even without eyes she had a clear sense of the place. She could "hear the color," "see the sound," "feel the imbalance," lyrical metaphors for trusting not people but the environment. She could never get those little phrases out of her head, probably because they had been beaten into her so well. Her old drill instructor spoke in poetry and punched in prose. "The lie of sight," he loved to remind her. "Trust your nose, trust your gut—your eyes will get you killed."

The black sack over her head was designed to keep out the light, to obscure the one sense most easily fooled. That was fine. She rarely believed her eyes anyway: a lesson well learned. Her most primal sense, the one wired straight into the lizard part of her brain, smelled the fear. The smell told her she was screwed. It also told her she was not alone.

As to the why, that question had barely made its way into her consciousness. How she had been nabbed, bagged, and dumped into this place was something she could scarcely get her head around.

She knew that there were only a few people she knew capable of taking her by surprise, let alone subduing her—and they were dead.

But the *who* and the *why* would have to wait; her training and her gut told her that now was about just staying alive.

As she lay on a hard floor, her honed senses of smell and hearing told her there was more than one person in the room: both men and women. The women were easy to detect. There were two different perfumes in the air, just enough fragrance for her nose to pick them out of the mixed scents of sweat, fear, and urine. Clearly not military. Civilian? *What the hell were civilians doing here?*

The men were also easy to sense. The movement she heard around her felt nervous, skittish, the kind of motions dogs make when they are caged and pace back and forth. Women tend to stand still, consider things, be less twitchy. Also, the sour breath and general man-stink was recognizable anywhere: in training barracks, in the field, or in the dark with a hood over your head.

There was also the smell of iron and the tang of blood in the air: fresh blood. Her blood she knew, as she pulled on the cords cutting into the flesh of her ankles and wrists. Of course, it was her blood. Good lubricant: she could eventually use it to work her hands free. She might have to break a bone or two in one of her hands in order to slip through the ties, but she'd done it before; she could do it again. If she lived long enough to try.

They were close, too close. She could hear their breathing, rapid, high in their chests, bodies geared for emotional flight but with nowhere to go. One breathing pattern was different. A woman maybe, but no—this one smelled like a male, his breathing deeper, steady breaths. Perhaps more training than the others, and he was focused on her. He was behind her, to the right. She would have to take him first. Suddenly someone grabbed the bag and a clump of her hair and pulled quickly, removing both.

Her head jerked back with the pull and the pain. She remained face down. A bright, searing light blinded her. Not the clean light of day but the dirty, green light of bad fluorescence. Just as she thought: indoors, enclosed, imprisoned. Someone knelt in front of her.

One of the women. She squinted and raised her eyes to see.

Now she got a look at part of the room. White floor, white walls, empty. There was a video monitor embedded in a far wall and next to it an old-fashioned digital clock that looked more like an old-fashioned, oversized alarm clock. But the face showed "00:00:00" in deep red numbers. Why a clock—not a clock, a timer? And the woman, blond, hair pulled back into a messy ponytail, wearing jeans and a frumpy blouse.

"Hey. I'm Ruby. I'm not going to hurt you. I can undo your hands and feet. Would you like to sit up? Might be more comfortable." Ruby leaned forward, grabbed her by the shoulders and gently lifted her off the floor to a sitting position. Ruby leaned down close enough that she could have used her mouth to rip out Ruby's throat. But then what? She was still tied up like a calf at a Texas rodeo. She did not resist. The time would come. Right now, she at least had a better tactical view. Her survival percentage had just increased substantially.

"Ruby—back off! Don't be stupid!" The man with the slower breathing was hostile, had a British accent and a commanding voice. The others, one woman and two men backed up a couple of paces.

"Don't be silly, Tully. She's fine. She's just scared like the rest of us. Like you were when you were thrown in here bound with a bag on your head." Ruby's voice was surprisingly centered for someone scared. She was resisting Tully's authority, not in-your-face rebellion but resisting.

Whoever they were, they were not a trained team or coordinated in any way. All prisoners? Yes, they were all captives. This changed things considerably.

Ruby finished untying her hands and feet, and helped her to sit up, and then gently backed off to a safe distance. She ignored Tully but still had some caution in her. She was beginning to like this Ruby. There was strength in her.

"What I was, Ruby dear, was bloody pissed off. I was not scared. Let us all be clear on that, thank you very much." Tully harrumphed and sat in one of the plastic chairs to pout, crossing his arms across his chest defiantly.

Finally she had a clear view of the room and all of its occupants. The room was rectangular, maybe thirty feet wide and twenty feet long. Everything was white: floors, walls, ceiling. The worn, white tiles of the floor extended halfway up each of the walls. The monitor and timer hung on one wall but nothing else. The room was sealed, except for a single door at the far end. A door with no knob. Five white plastic chairs were strewn around the room, the cheap kind you can buy at neighborhood garden shops or home improvement box stores. And there were cameras, embedded in the ceiling so you couldn't knock them out or disable them, say with a hard blow from a cheap plastic chair. She had no doubt that room's resemblance to a butcher's shop was not accidental.

Ruby leaned down and offered her hand. "Hi. I'm Ruby," she giggled. "Sorry, I'm repeating myself. I just told you my name. I'm from California." The others watched, unsure, cautious, waiting. Ruby stood her ground, keeping eye contact: she was going to get that handshake, that was clear. If she refused the handshake, then the group would never trust her. It would be seen as a symbolic "up yours," and she would get no cooperation from any of them if she needed it. Not shaking set up a potentially adversarial relationship, but it also showed she was independent, a leader. This might prove valuable later on. If there was a later on. Shaking, on the other hand, showed a sense of unity, inclusion, *I'm one of you*. Unity might be the only thing that would keep both her and them alive. She looked at Ruby and the others with calculating eyes. They were all scared, except Tully. He was bored. He was going to be a problem. The choice was clear.

She reached up and took Ruby's hand. "Mae."

Ruby used the handshake to help Mae stand up, "See, I don't bite." From the sidelines Tully chimed in, "It's not you she should be worried about, is it?"

A middle-aged African American man stepped up. "Michael, Cleveland, Ohio."

Then, a fifty-something Indian. "Sanjay, Mumbai, India."

A thirtyish hipster with a thick Mandarin accent got

right up into Mae's face. Her grip was strong and her gaze defiant, "Ling, New York City. Why do people introduce themselves and then say where they're from? Who the fuck cares?"

Mae gave back what she got, "I don't." She let go and smirked as she walked away.

Everyone looked at Tully, waiting for him to get up and play nice: no such luck. While lying trussed up on the floor, Mae had been the outlier. Now, everyone was on Mae's side of the room, and Tully was alone in his chair, every bit outside looking in. It was clear from the look on his face that he recognized a new dynamic was forming. He got up and moved tentatively toward the others. Mae smiled to herself. *Nobody likes being on the outside—except me.*

Mae spoke directly to him. "What did you mean?"

"Mean? About what?" Tully replied. There may have been a question mark at the end of his reply, but it wasn't a question.

"When you suggested Ruby wasn't the one with the teeth I should be afraid of."

Tully laughed. "Did you get a look at that goon that brought you here?"

"No. I had a bag over my head!"

"We all had bags over our heads," Ling interjected.

Tully ignored Ling and focused on Mae. "Where were you when they took you?"

This Mae remembered well. When it happened it had been fast, quiet, painful, and faceless. Whoever did this to her knew her skill set and exactly how to take her out. Something like this had only happened to her once before in her life, during the war, and she promised herself *never again*. So much for promises.

Granted, she had to admit that this time there was no reason to have her guard up, but that's always when the unexpected happened in her line of work—when you're sleeping, having sex, taking a shower, or in her case putting groceries into the trunk of a car. An old Ford Econoline van pulled up behind her, its door slid open, and two freakishly tall men dressed in black coveralls and combat boots jumped out and came toward her in a rush. She remembered their movements as beautifully synchronized, ballet-like; their timing impeccable, and their execution flawless.

Even in the midst of being mugged, she appreciated well-trained machines. She should know; she used to be just like them. Trapped between her car and theirs (obviously part of the plan), there was nothing to do but kick testicles and gouge eyes out. But her kicking met nothing fleshy. Instead, the top of her shoe slammed into tight muscle and bone, nearly breaking her foot. *Did these guys have their junk removed?* As for her simultaneous attack to their eyes, the men wore goggles of a type she'd never seen before. They were perfect protection and resisted even her hardest punches or attempts to pull them off. Two massive hulks loomed over her and then pulled out a prod of some kind—another implement she could not identify but soon felt.

She had been tasered before, but this was different. She had even been full-out electrocuted, by drug lords in Bolivia, but this was not that either. The feeling was like nothing she had ever felt, and she felt it for less time than it took for them to touch her with the weapons. She barely had time to formulate a final thought before everything vanished into the oblivion of unconsciousness. *Who are these guys?*

～

Order on Amazon:
https://amzn.to/2v8J9Ra
(also available in paperback, e-book, audiobook)

One room. Six People. No way out. And every 13 minutes one of them dies—horribly—unless they can figure out what their nameless, faceless, and creepily mysterious captor wants from them. One woman holds the key to their survival or deaths. But, only if she faces her own bloody past and the earth-shattering truth of why they are all trapped together. Her final choice to own the truth can bring freedom or oblivion—13 little minutes will tell the tale—for all of humanity.

[SEE NEXT PAGE]

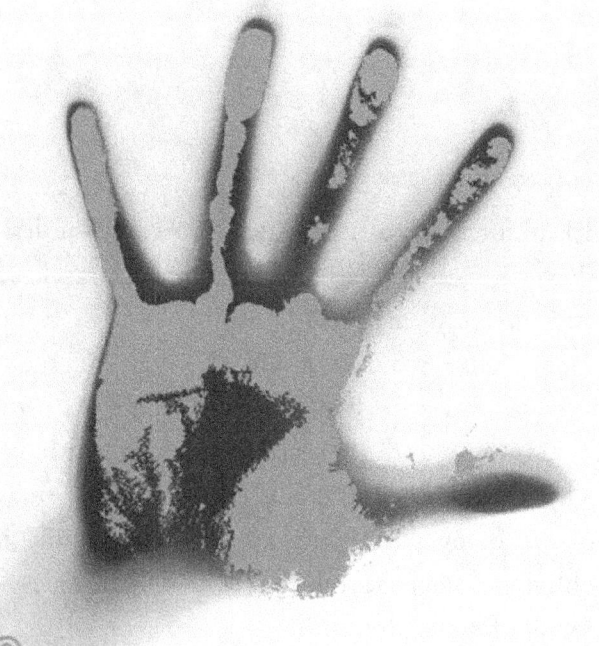

a novella

13 MINUTES

JEFF LYONS

ALSO BY JEFF LYONS

FICTION

Jack Be Dead: Revelation (bk #1)

13 Minutes

Terminus Station

NONFICTION

Anatomy of a Premise Line: How to Use Story and Premise Development for Writing Success

Rapid Story Development: How to Use the Enneagram-Story Connection to Become a Master Storyteller

Rapid Story Development: The Storyteller's Toolbox Volume One

RAPID STORY DEVELOPMENT E-BOOK SERIES

#1: Commercial Pace in Fiction and Creative Nonfiction

#2: Bust the Top Ten Creative Writing Myths to Become a Better Writer

#3: Ten Questions Every Writer Needs to Ask Before They Hire a Consultant

#4: Teams and Ensembles: How to Write Stories with Large Casts

#5: The Moral Premise–How to Build a Bulletproof

Narrative Engine for Any Story

#6: Seven Steps to Busting Writer's Block Forever

ABOUT THE AUTHOR

Jeff Lyons is a published author and story consultant with more than 25 years of experience in the publishing and entertainment industries. He has worked with literally thousands of screenwriters and novelists, including *New York Times* and *USA Today* bestselling authors. His writings on the craft of storytelling can be found in leading trade magazines like *Writer's Digest Magazine*, *Script Magazine*, and *The Writer Magazine*, among others. His book, *Anatomy of a Premise Line: How to Master Premise and Story Development for Writing Success* was published by Focal Press in 2015. Jeff is a popular presenter at leading writing industry trade conferences, and has been invited to present and consult for the annual Producers Guild of America's "Power of Diversity Producers Fellowship Program," as well as for the Film Independent Screenwriting Lab. Jeff lives in Long Beach, California, has one weird cat, and desperately wants a dog. Visit www.storygeeks.com.

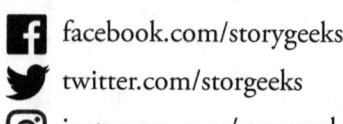

facebook.com/storygeeks

twitter.com/storgeeks

instagram.com/storygeeks